A Steamy BWWM Romance
Volume 1

Jada Washington

Copyright

Table of Contents

Homecoming

"Have you gotten a date for prom yet?"

"No, not yet. What about you?" I asked my friend, Becca Lawrence.

She closed her locker and grinned, "Yep, Patrick Foles asked me. I didn't want to say anything until you found a date."

"Oh…" I looked down and clutched my textbooks to my chest tighter. Suddenly the temperature in the school felt like it was thousand degrees.

Becca frowned and touched my shoulder. "I wouldn't fret if someone hasn't asked you yet. Is there a guy you hope that would ask you, Mariah?"

"I was hoping that Peter might ask me out."

"Peter McRoy? Oh, you and him, go way back since middle school! I am surprised he hadn't asked you either. I saw the way you two were cuddling up on the bus back from the weekend's track meet. I don't buy the whole, sharing earbuds thing either. He likes you. He just wanted to use your headphones to get close to you."

"Yeah?" I gave my friend of eight years a guilty smile. "Did I ever tell you that I have a crush on him?"

"Oh my god! No, you don't!"

"Yeah. I mean who wouldn't like him? He's captain of the track team. He's an honor student, not to mention, have you seen him in his track shorts. Oh, lord!"

Becca laughed as she followed me towards A.P Chemistry.

As we climbed the stairs she asked, "do you think he's going to ask you?"

"I'm not sure. I mean, I know he hasn't asked anyone else out yet."

"That's strange. He's a good-looking guy. I'm sure he has to have one or two girls on his mind."

"Yeah, that's what I'm worried about."

We stopped outside the class and I placed my back on a locker nearby. The minute bell rang, and I frowned knowing that my conversation with my friend would end soon.

"If he doesn't ask you, why don't you ask him?"

"What do you mean? Girls don't ask the guys."

"It's not the 90s anymore, Mariah. Woman are progressive now. Hell, we may have a woman president if Hilary beats Obama in the primaries. All I'm saying is, ditch the dated views of the past. Ask him out. He likes you. You like him. It's as simple as that."

"Oh, I don't know. What if he says no."

"Then that's the worst thing that is going to happen. If it does, and I'm not saying it will, but if it does, you pick yourself up and you go stag. You'll have fun with me and Patrick."

"Are you sure?"

"Yes."

The second bell rang, and Becca and I shared the same glance. As we ran to our seats, she whispered in my ear, "trust me it will all work out in the end."

I couldn't take my eyes off him. Watching him stretch was the best part of my day. Him bending over in short shorts should be considered XXX rated. Watching the hem of his shorts rise, showing his tone pale thighs was a godsend. Not to mention the bulge in his shorts. While I've never seen a real male's penis, I imagine his to be big. Perhaps after prom, Peter and I could rent a hotel room and spend our first time together. Hell, everyone was doing it, Becca was planning on hooking up with Patrick that night, why couldn't we?

Just thinking of having sex with Peter made my insides quiver. The way he held himself was so damn hot. Surrounding him were his friends. He must had said a funny joke as they laughed and goofed off. Behind me, I heard Coach Owens blow his whistle and shout it was time for warmups and everyone started to run around the track at a slow pace. As I ran, I caught up to Peter and nudged him on the shoulder.

"Hey."

"Hey yourself," he grinned.

"How's your day going?"

"I got an 80 on my English report, so I wouldn't say it's bad. What about you?"

"Normal day at Green Valley High. Hey, so I had a question."

"Shoot."

"Have you asked anyone out to the dance?"

"No, has anyone asked you yet?"

"Nope. Still single."

I noticed a small smile creep on his face. Seeing it gave me hope that perhaps Becca was right about him.

"Did you might want to..."

A loud whistle interrupted my thoughts as I saw Coach Owens glare at us. "Hustle it up you two! This ain't social hour. We got Greenville High this week everyone should be focused! That means you Matthews!"

I rolled my eyes and Peter and I both picked up our pace.

"What were you going to ask me?" He whispered.

"Never mind. I don't want to give Coach Owens a heart attack because our lack of hustle. We'll talk more after practice."

***

I waited outside the boy's locker room and Peter came strolling out. Gone was the short shorts and T-shirt, and instead he was wearing a hoodie and baggy jeans, with his book-bag strapped to his shoulder. His brown hair was slick back from his shower, and he smelled like old spice deodorant. Regardless of what he was wearing, he still looked sexy as hell. When he saw me he grinned.

"Hey, Mariah. Thanks for waiting for me."

"Anytime."

We walked out of the gym together, heading towards both of our cars. The parking lot was mostly empty as most high schoolers and teachers had left for the day. After sharing a few glances and smiles, Peter asked me, "so what did you want to talk to me about?"

"It's about prom." I looked down and bit my lip. "You said earlier that you don't have a date, right?"

"Yeah."

I looked back at him and played around with my bag strap. My breathing increased and my mouth suddenly felt dry. As I stumbled to find my words, I was beginning to understand why guys were nervous when they asked a girl out.

"Do you...perhaps...want...to go with...?"

"To prom?" He asked.

"Yeah?"

"Sure. Honestly, I was planning on asking you."

"Seriously?"

"Yeah."

"Oh my god! This is great news! I can't believe it. Oh my god. I...I...Ah!"

Without thinking I jumped into his arms and kissed him. Mid kiss, Peter pushed me away and his eyes were as big as saucers as he stared at me.

"Whoa!" He claimed as he combed his fingers through his brown hair.

"Sorry. To much?" I back away, slacked jawed. I felt stupid for kissing him. In my mind, I was screaming why did I do that.

"No, not at all." Peter grinned, grabbed my waist, and pulled me back towards him. Our lips connected once more as we shared our first inmate kiss.

Becca and Patrick were inseparable walking to A.P chem. Lost were the five-minute girl time talks, now replaced with five minute make out sessions between the two. I honestly wasn't jealous. I had my own man meat. Our five minute make out times were set after track practice near our cars.

God, I loved kissing Peter. The way his lips felt, gliding across mine. They felt perfect, like two puzzle pieces coming together. Kissing him was so amazing that, I'd forget that time existed.

Our relationship was nearly perfect, except for the fact that I've never met his parents. Every time we'd hung out it was either at my house or at the mall with Becca and Patrick. I found it annoying that I still haven't gone over to his house or had dinner with his parents, but I never pressed the issue.

After dropping Patrick off at his Pre-Calc. class, Becca and I double timed it to A.P Chem hoping not to be late.

As we sped walked, Becca asked me, "so I've made plans with my parents. They're getting us a limo and made reservations for us at a Japanese Steakhouse."

Figures, unlike me, Becca's family is loaded. They have more cash than they know what to do with it. While her summers are spent lounging by her backyard pool, I'm sweating like a pig at the local fast food joint getting burned by grease to help my parents pay rent.

"Becca..."

"I know what your thinking, don't worry about it. They told me to tell you not to worry about the cost for the limo. You just have to pay for your portion of the dinner."

"Awesome. Thanks for setting this all up."

"You kidding me? You only get one senior prom. After this we will be living our lives at college then getting jobs. Who knows when we will see each other again?"

"Don't say that. We both got accepted into State. We're going to be roommates and get into our normal shenanigans on campus. We're going to be friends forever. Hell, our kids might be friends too."

Becca laughed and rolled her eyes.

"You're crazy. Did I ever tell you that?"

I laughed and shrugged. "Speaking of crazy. We're you able to get rooms at the hotel?"

"Yeah, but there's some bad news attached."

"Oh, boy. What's the good news?"

"Good news is that Patrick's older brother hooked us up. He got us two rooms for the night. Bad news is that you owe him two hundred for it."

"Two hundred!" I shouted.

"Yeah, I guess hotel rooms aren't cheap."

"Shit, I guess so. I never realized that my parents pay so much for a room. Could you cover me till summer? That's when I start working again. I'll pay you back, I promise."

"Yeah sure. I got you girl."

"And remember our lies to our parents. We're sleeping over at each other's houses."

"Got it."

We made it to the lab classroom before the minute bell and we stopped to stand outside by the lockers. Taking out her makeup mirror, Becca checked her lip gloss before looking back at me.

"Mariah, I never asked you, what colors are you and Peter wearing?"

"Well, I bought an orange dress because, Peter likes that color."

"That's a weird color."

"Yeah, I know. I don't even look good in orange, but Peter likes it and I like him, so there were no questions asked."

The minute bell rang signaling the end of our conversation and as we walked into the classroom to take our seats, Becca whispered to me, "That's good that you like him. You two are a perfect couple."

I grinned and said, "Thanks, girl."

***

"Peter!" I shouted as I ran up to him. I jumped into his arms and gave him a big kiss. However, my passion wasn't equally reciprocated. He placed me back down, with a large frown on his face. His eyes were filled with pain and emotion.

"Peter whats wrong?"

"We're done." He growled

"What?"

"You and I are breaking up." He muttered, walking away.

"Peter? What's going on. This isn't funny. If this is some sort of prank..."

"It's not, okay?" His voice grew louder, and his fists balled together.

"What the hell, Peter? I thought we loved each other. That night after mall, we..."

"I was wrong. I don't love you. We're through." Peter turned around and opened the door to his pickup truck. He tossed his bag in and walked towards the driver's side.

I stood frozen in place, in shock of the unexpected break up. In my head, I kept repeating that this wasn't real.

"Peter..." I found myself saying. I chased after him and grabbed his hand. "Peter wait! What's changed? Yesterday we couldn't keep our hands off each other and today you're pushing me away? Something is wrong, tell me!"

When Peter turned around, I saw the tears falling down his face. His eyes were red, and he looked to be emotional wounded.

"I..." he stuttered. He held my hand and stared in my eyes. I could tell he wanted to tell me something. There was conflict in his heart. He reached up and touched my cheek. We stared into each other's eyes before he shook his head and backed away. "No, no, no, I'm sorry. I can't."

"Can't what? Peter please. Help me understand. Why are you doing this."

"I..." he looked down then towards the football stadium, avoiding my eyes. "I found someone else." He finally admitted.

"What?"

"I've found someone else. I've cheated on you and I've asked someone else to the dance. I don't love you anymore."

"No, Peter. That's not true. I don't believe you."

His eyes met mine again. He looked beaten and bruised as if our conversation was sucking the life force from him.

"It's true. We're through." He growled. He turned and hopped into his truck, slamming the door.

"Peter wait!" But before I could get another word out, Peter spun out his tires leaving me in the dust. As I watched his taillights leave the school, I fell to my knees in tears.

Chapter 4
(Prom Night, April 25, 2008)

I didn't know why I was there. I was stuck going stag with my friend and her boyfriend. I was stuck in the awkward third wheel position as I was dragged from place to place in a limo. I was stuck in an ugly orange dress, matching no one. I was stuck in my own head. The entire night was a bust. I hated my life.

My parents were the ones who forced me out of the house, claiming that I'll only get one prom and I should enjoy it. Personally, I would have rather stayed home in my pajamas watching reruns of Lost, but neither or less I was there. Forced to live my worst nightmare. Forced to wear this stupid dress. Forced to watch my ex boyfriend grind and dance on this mystery whore he'd taken to the prom.

Speaking of the whore, I still haven't met her. Every time I saw Peter in the hallway at school he would always turn around. He actively avoided me on the track team, by either running ahead of me or sitting in a different section of the bus. But all of that was okay. I'm still feeling wounded from our breakup. I'm not sure how he feels, but the whole idea of dating and high school was dumb, and I was over it.

All and all, I'm through with this stage of my life. I've already decided that I'm not going to State with Becca. Although I love her to death, she's just another reminder of him. I'd decided to pack my bags and head to across the country to California to attend UCLA. I'm done with North Carolina, there's nothing here for me but pain and suffering.

"Hey, earth to Mariah. Earth to Mariah." Becca called out waving her hand.

"Huh, What?"

"What's up with you?"

"Nothing. I'm just thinking?"

"Thinking about what?" She asked.

"I don't know Becca! Why do you care so much!" I snapped. I crossed my arms and looked out the window. I was through with talking to anyone. All I wanted to do was go home. Just seeing Becca and Patrick happy made my blood boil.

"I care because you don't look so good. You got BRF."

Patrick laughed and I glared at him. Watching him laugh made me want to punch him.

"BRF?" I growled.

"Bitch resting face. Listen, girl, I know things aren't going your way, but it's prom. You should be excited. We only get…"

"If you say we only get one prom, I'm going to lose it."

"Sorry, but it's true. You shouldn't let him ruin this time. Throughout the night you've been moping around. Through pictures at my parents, through dinner, even now on the drive there. I could be a bitch and ignore this and have a good time with Patrick, but I'm not. I'm concerned about you. You only get one time to be a teenager. No, do overs. So, what if Peter dumped you for some other slut. You woman up, keep your head up, and push on. You are a strong woman and you…"

"Becca I…"

"Save it," she snapped. Her eyes narrowed and she reached across the limo to hold my hand. "You listen here, Mariah Matthews." The fire in her eyes was intense. I'd never seen her with such emotion.

"You are a strong beautiful woman. Repeat it."

"Becca…I"

"REPEAT IT!" She yelled. Her facial expressions were filled with a teary-eyed passion that I'd never seen before. She was through with my shit and she wasn't playing anymore games.

"I'm a strong beautiful woman," I muttered.

"Louder!" She roared. "Let the fuckin driver know that your proud. Hell, let everyone driving on the highway know who's in this fucking limo."

"I'm a strong beautiful woman!" I screamed.

A smile cracked on Becca's face as she held my hand. "Thata girl. You're my ride and die chick. I ain't going to let anything happen to you tonight. If that whore that Peter is with says something or looks at you, I got your back got it? I don't care if we get suspended. That bitch will get slapped if she tries to step to us, right?" She grinned.

"Right," I replied, feeling a smile grow on my face. I nodded, feeling a new sense of energy from my friend.

The rest of the drive I felt confident. My chest was up, and I held a smile thinking that the prom wouldn't be so bad. However, I was wrong the minute I stepped into the hotel's banquet room. From across the room, I saw him. Orange bow tie and all, and my heart melted. I forgot to breathe, and my legs turned into jello. Just like that I was back to my moping self.

"I think I'll go get some punch."

"We just got here. Don't you want to dance a little first?" Becca asked me.

"No, I'm thirsty."

Becca nodded then noticed Peter in the corner of the room eyeballing us. She shook her head and before I could walk away, she grabbed my hand.

"Remember what I said. You're a strong beautiful woman. After you're done getting a drink, find us on the dance floor, okay?"

I nodded and gave her fake smile. My heart burned lying to my best friend. I wasn't a strong woman. I was weak.

When we separated, I walked to the refreshment table and pour myself a glass of punch. After my first sip, I heard Peter behind me.

"Hey Mariah. How's the punch?" He asked nervously. He grabbed the ladle and poured himself a glass as well. My hands clutched the paper cup tighter as I thought about throwing it in his face.

"Getting juice for your slut?" I sneered.

"No, it's for me."

I looked around the hall trying to find the woman that Peter might bring to the prom.

"So, where is she? Where's this woman you cheated on me with?"

"Well...that's what I wanted to talk to you about. I wanted to apologize. I didn't..."

"You didn't what, Peter? Think about my feelings when you broke my heart? Think about how lonely I felt watching my best friend and her boyfriend be together on a romantic trip to the prom. Think about how my heart felt after you ripped it in two? No, Peter you didn't think."

"Please. I made a mistake. Just let my explain."

"Damn right you made a mistake. Ugh! What did I see you in? I can't believe I loved you! Not to mention, I wanted to sleep with you! All of this time, it was just a ploy to take my virginity wasn't it!" My voice grew louder the more I stared at Peter. Just looking at him reignited a fire.

"No, Mariah. Please, just listen to me. I love you, but..."

"But what Peter? You can't love someone then cheat behind their back."

I could feel more and more eyes stare at us the louder I got. Peter could feel the same as his shoulders slumped and he leaned closer to me.

"Mariah, could you please lower your voice. Perhaps I could take you outside and we can..."

"We can what, Peter? The whole school deserves to know that Peter McRoy is an asshole. No, Fuck you Peter, we're through."

I took my drink and tossed in his face. The entire class reacted to my outburst but didn't care. The world now knew that Peter McRoy was a loser. I was done with him and done with the school. While he stood wiping the red juice from his eyes, I flicked him off and walked out of the door with my head held high.

"Fuck this place. I'm done with this school and I'm done with Peter McRoy." I screamed, pushing the doors open.

It's been ten years since I've been in Green Valley, North Carolina. After graduation, I went against my promise and didn't got to college with Becca. I left my best friend in the wind and moved to the West Coast to attend UCLA. I left her to become a lawyer and the youngest person in my firm to become partner. At the time, I thought I was leaving for myself, but now I realized I only left because I was selfish. When I threw away my life in North Carolina, I didn't realize that I left her when she needed me most. Now ten years later, I'm face to face with her once again, but this time she's not smiling back at me. Hell, I can't even see her beautiful face because the accident left her body militated. Even though I couldn't see her, I could still imagine her bright smile from high school.

I sat in the second row of the funeral as the first row was saved for family. I recognized her mom, who always used to pick us up from school, her dad, who taught me how to shoot a gun, and her younger brother who Becca and I used to torture growing up. All of them looked older and and depressed as their brightest star just went black. Upon thinking about it, I realized that this was the first time I'd ever seen any of them cry. Watching the tears fall down their faces made me tear up again. Goddamn, I miss her.

Included in the row where three other faces I knew nothing about. I only knew their faces from Facebook. After prom, I stopped talking to Becca. Like me she went to college, however that's when our lives got different. She met Kyle at State. They fell in love, got married, had two kids. Each one of those milestones, I wasn't apart of. It was dumb to ignore her.

Even when I was at my lowest, she wasn't. She didn't stop sending me letters and presents. Even when I didn't send her anything, she would still keep in contact. It wasn't until last week when I got a text from my mom with a link to the obituaries. Seeing her bright smile, in a list full of death and sadness twisted and squeezed my heart liked I've never felt before. I cried in my office the entire day. She was so young to be taken away. Hit by a driver, twice over the drinking limit. She died, he didn't. I hope the motherfucker burns in hell.

Without thinking I booked a flight to Green Valley, the one place I swore I'll never returned too. Four hours later, I'm sitting here watching my best friend get lowered into the dirt.

The entire funeral was filled with memories of Becca and me. I thought about all of our times spent together and the fun that we had. I was in a shell of my own self until I felt someone touch my shoulder.

"Mariah?"

I turned to see a Becca's husband. His eyes were red, and he held a soft smile.

"I'm Kyle. Becca's..." he looked down and sobbed again as he received another reminder of what he lost.

"Hey, Kyle. It's good to finally meet you. Becca's told me a lot about you, Matthew, and Jasmine."

"That's good to hear. Becca talked about you a lot too. You two got in a lot of trouble back in high school."

I laughed. "More than you know." My body shuddered as I felt emotional again.

He smiled and hugged me. The way he wrapped my arms around my shoulders felt like a warm blanket. I really needed a hug.

"She would be so happy to know you came. Thank you for coming," He whispered in my ear.

"I'm sorry. I'm so sorry that I didn't..." I couldn't finish the words. I broke down and cried in his arms.

"The guilt was the worst part." I sobbed into his shoulder. "If I would have known that his would happened, I would have..."

"Shhh..." Kyle comforted, rubbing my back. "You didn't know. Do not do that yourself. It would only make this worse. Becca wouldn't want that. She told me about the strong woman you have become. Keep your head up."

I smiled at his words. He sounded just like Becca. "Thanks, Kyle." We broke apart and I wiped my face.

"Before I get called away, Becca had a letter for you in her will. You don't have to read this here, but know what ever she wrote, she still loved you till the day she died."

I smiled and hugged him once more. "Thanks, Kyle."

Kyle and I talked for a little while longer. I told him more stories of Becca and he seemed to like them. It wasn't until he was called away by someone else that he left, and I suddenly felt more a lone than I ever had in my life. I sat there poking at some cake from the celebration of life when I heard my name once more, accept, this was from a voice I recognized. It was Peter McRoy.

The skinny track star from my youth was replaced by a muscular bound hunk. For a second, I nearly forgot why I hated him as I stared at his perfectly parted hair. Damn did he look gorgeous, like fucking model gorgeous. I've seen some celebrities in LA, but damn he put each one to shame. But seeing him was also a reminder that he and me were through. Like Becca, he probably moved on with his life. Looking at his sexy matured body, I knew some woman had snatched him up, put a ring on him and tied him down with two kids and a mortgage. However, the longer I stared, the more memories of him and I filtered through. It must have been the funeral because memories of us flooded my mind. Just thinking of him, made my mouth dry.

"Mariah, I thought I saw you."

I backed away. I looked left and right, searching for an exit. I had to run.

"Mariah wait, I just want to say hello. That's all." He held his hands up. I noticed his left hand was bare and ring less.

Was he not married, I thought. I shook my head at the possibly and backed away.

"Mariah, wait."

"You said hello, Peter and there's nothing more to say."

"Mariah!" He called out but I was already my way out the door. I didn't think I could cry any more than I could, but I already felt the tears rolled down my cheeks. Hopping in the car, I slammed the door and all the emotions that I'd spend years burying remerged in seconds. Just then I thought about Becca and what she would have told me. Needing her words, I opened the letter that Kyle gave me and read it silently.

Dear Mariah,

Hey girl, I miss you. I know we haven't spent much time together, but you've had such an impact on my life that words couldn't express it. I love you and miss you.

I know this is morbid, reading a letter from your dead best friend, but preparing my will gave me the idea to do this. Over the years, I've tried multiple times to explain to you the situation with Peter, and you've shut me down every time. However, now that I'm dead, it's your time to listen. No more games. While Peter's to blame for breaking up with you, you should know it wasn't his idea. It was his parents. They got wind of you two dating and let's just say that their views aren't as progressive as their son's. When they caught wind that he was dating a black woman and taking her to prom, they wanted him to break up with you immediately. They forced him to do it. He never cheated on you. He didn't bring a date to the prom with him. He went stag, just like you. While he made the mistake of dumping you, you have to understand why he did it.

For an 18 year old kid, you can't imagine the pressure of telling your parents to fuck off. He was scared. He was trapped in a decision he was too young to make. He made a mistake. Forgive him about it.

I know he still hasn't. I also know that he still has eyes for you. He's grown man now, Mariah, not the scared boy who dumped you. He's also single. You should tap that. Seriously, the man is a God.

P.S Kyle if you are snooping and reading this, I mean no offense to you. You are the love of my life, but Peter is some man meat reserved for Mariah. Babe, if I do die between now and the time of this letter and Peter McRoy is still single, pass this note to Mariah. Let her know that even on this darkest day, there's still hope for love.

I love you guys,

Becca

I reread the letter several times. Each time I felt the wave of emotion crash into me. I stayed in my car crying until day turned to night and several others were walking out to their cars. I was rereading the letter for the thirteenth time when I heard a knock at my door. Looking up, I saw it was Peter with a smile.

"Hey are you alright? I thought you left, but I guess..."

"Is it true? I blurted.

"What?"

"Is it true you dumped me because of your parents."

Peter narrowed his eyes. "Who told you?"

"Becca. In this letter." I showed him the paper and he stared at it. After a second of silence, he nodded.

"Yes, it's true. Ten years ago, I made a mistake. I mistake that I'd never left myself forget."

"Why didn't you tell me?"

"I tired, on several occasions, but you've always shut me down."

"Why are still single?"

"I don't know." He looked down and rubbed the back of his head. "It's not like I haven't tried. It's just that..." He closed his eyes then reopened them to stare in mine with a fiery passion. "I haven't felt the same without you. You were my first and only love."

"Is it strange to say that I feel the same?" I asked with a smile. I shook my head and replied, "I can't believe it's taken a friends death to say this, but not a moment goes on where I don't think of you. I still you love too, Peter."

A smile cracked over his face, as he leaned closer to me. He cupped my chin and rubbed my cheek. His passionate eyes stared into mine. My heart was moving triple it's normal pace. Our surroundings seemed to freeze in place as it was only him and me in the parking lot. Leaning closer, I saw him stare at my lips and I instantly knew what he wanted.

A kiss.

It's been ten years, and I should have pushed him away, but I couldn't. I couldn't turn my back again. I had to see where this road of him and I led. I place my hand on his broad chest and nodded.

"It's okay. I want to..."

Before I could say another word, Peter stuck his head through my window and kissed me. The feeling of this smooth lips dancing across my own took me back. Back when we're two kids on the track team making out by our cars. The way his tongue danced across my own felt erotic and passionate. I'd never felt a spark like I did with Peter. His kiss was one of a million and felt like an idiot for denying myself the pleasure. We must have kissed for minutes until we broke apart breathless.

"So now what?" He asked.

"I want you to prove to me how much you've grown. Dinner, me and you at your parents house."

"Deal, on one exception."

"Which is…"

"We pick up where we left off. We're dating now." Peter declared.

"Okay."

Peter broke a smile and bent down to kiss me once more.

I pulled up the rental car to Peter's house and took a deep breath. Like Becca, Peter lived in the nice part of town, filled with golf courses and country clubs. Parking in the driveway of the mansion, I could tell why Peter always had traveling money for our away meets. Walking to the door, I thought about our past relationship. Since our kiss, I'd extended my vacation with my job and spent most of time with him. We've reconnected and I've learned that he's now a high school teacher and a track coach. I'd never saw him as a teacher. The fact that he had roots gave me pause about our new relationship. Working as a teacher is a lot harder to uproot your life for a long-distance relationship. While we talked about a potential relationship, I made it clear that nothing was set in stone until I met his parents. If he was truly a different man than he was ten years ago he should be able tell his parents that he's in an interracial relationship with a black woman.

I rung the doorbell and Peter greeted me. He was wearing a nice button-down shirt and jeans. His sleeves were rolled up and he looked like a professional model for Abercrombie. Knowing he'd dressed for the occasion, I attempted to look like his twin. I was wearing a grey sweater along with a pencil skirt and heels. Upon looking at me, his eyes sparkled.

"Mariah...you look stunning." He gave me a quick peck and a hug.

"Thanks Peter. So, do you."

He smiled then nodded his head inside.

"Well, come on in."

Peter led me through the large home, through the foyer, past the living room to the open roomed kitchen. There I spotted his parents. His dad was sitting in a bar stool while his mother cooked what looked like prime rib.

"Mom, Dad, this is Mariah." Peter introduced.

"Hello," I greeted waving my hand. "I brought wine. I didn't know what you liked so I picked up a Chardonnay."

"Oh, well isn't that nice," Peter's mom said, looking at the bottle. "It's nice to meet you Mariah. I'm Martha and that's my husband, Wayne. We'll put it over here." She placed the wine on the counter and smiled back towards me.

It was one of those fake smiles that seemed like there were imaginary fingers spreading her lips wide. "You know Mariah, a red wine would be better for tonight," Wayne explained.

"Is there a difference? Wine is wine right?" I joked.

"Red goes well with prime rib. Do black people even eat prime rib?"

"Dad!" Peter snapped.

"What? It's just a question."

"Dad please..."

I gave Peter a look and realized why he might had held back on telling his parents of our relationship. Holding my head high, I replied, "black people do eat prime rib. I'm sorry about the wine choice. I wasn't aware that we were eating red meat."

Peter's dad rose an eyebrow but didn't say anything. He grumbled to himself and continued to read the paper.

"Sorry about that. My dad's a big wine person."

"That's okay. I'm sure it could be enjoyed on another occasion."

Peter nodded nervously and wiped his hands on his jeans. "Speaking of wine, lets open a bottle! Shall we?"

Insuring wine would break up the awkward silence in the room, I agreed with Peter. When Peter left the room to go to the wine cellar, the three of us got even more awkward.

"So, Mariah, what's it like on the west coast."

"It's nice. It's almost a completely different world compared to the East Coast."

"Huff. I bet. California filled with all those damn liberals and illegals. I'm amazed the state isn't on fire. Oh, wait it is," Wayne chuckled to himself and Martha giggled like a schoolgirl.

The joke felt like a personal attack. While I was born and raised in North Carolina, I've grown to love California and hearing him drag the states name in the mud made my blood boil.

"It's not all bad. California is a very diverse state with a healthy economy."

"Huh, that's not what I've heard."

Martha giggled again.

I closed my eyes and took a deep breath. If I hear her giggle on more damn time I was going to snap.

"Wayne, with all due respect, California has one of the highest GDPs in the country. We could practically be our own country."

"Then why haven't you? It would serve the entire nation a lot better without you people around."

"What you mean you people?"

"You know, free loaders, like yourself."

My blood was beginning to boil. My fist clenched and my teeth ground together.

"I am not a free loader. I worked my ass off. For a matter of fact, a lot of black people work their asses off."

"Oh dear, he wasn't referring to black people?" Martha added.

"Was he? I snapped back. "It certainly felt like it."

"I wasn't. I was simply implying the fact that you people on the west coast are lazy."

"There you go again using the phrase, you people. You keep using that phrase in a way to insult me."

"Mariah, would you calm down. My husband means no offense," Martha added.

"Really? No offense? I certainly feels like he's trying to offended me. I knew this meeting would be difficult, but seriously? For one day, you couldn't put aside your views for your son?"

"Our views?" Wayne asked, rising his eyebrows.

"Oh, don't act surprised. You've been rude to me since I've walked in the door. I've never been disrespected like I have in the last five minutes."

Martha giggled again and rolled her eyes. She whispered to herself and resumed cooking.

"What did you say?" I growled.

"What's that dear?"

"You whispered something to yourself. If you got something to say, how about you share it."

Martha looked at her husband then back at me. I could tell it was something bad, just by the look the two shared.

She sighed then said, "I was saying that I'm not sure what my son sees in you. Our assumptions were right about you. You clearly fly off the handle on small issues."

"Like racial prejudice? Yes, I'm going to fly off the handle about that. It's called respect, Martha."

Wayne stood out of his chair and glared at me. "That's enough!" he shouted. His voice shook the kitchen walls. "We have held back out tongues long enough. I will not have you come in here and disrespect my wife. We tried to be respectful to you, girl, but I see that you can't take the bitch out of the street. You have five seconds to leave my property, or so help me..."

"No, that's enough out of you!" Peter growled. His nostrils where flared, his eyes were wide open. Appearing from the cellar, his eyes glared at his father as if he was the devil himself. Not taking his eyes off his family, he pushed me behind his back as if to protect me.

"I heard the whole damn conversation downstairs. Not once did you accept her. You instead ridiculed her to the point that she had to fight back. Any human would. That's right, she might be a different color skin than me, dad, but I love her. I love her more than anything. I made a mistake in the past, one that I still have to make up for, but I will not make the same mistake again. Get your things, Mariah, were leaving."

"Peter..." Wayne began to say.

"Save it. You already said enough."

Peter helped me gather me things and as we walked out, Peter's mother pleaded, "Son, please, don't leave with her. Think about this..."

"I've thought about this for ten years, mother. You can't even bear a simple conversation with her. Perhaps in time we can try again, but not now. You need to learn that the woman I love is right here. I love Mariah and that fact, isn't debatable, it isn't exchangeable, nor is it ever going to change. No matter what you say or do."

Martha gasped as she looked at her husband for support.

Wayne growled and pointed towards the door. "If you walk out of that door, you are cut off. Do you hear me? Cut off, don't expect me to pay for anything."

"So, be it." Peter replied with a frown. "Goodbye, father." Peter grabbed the door handle and slapped it shut with a force that caused the whole house to shake.

Walking to the car, I was speechless at the man that defended me. I'd never expected in a million years to see Peter react that way.

"Peter...I'm sorry. I know that was hard and..."

Before I could say anything else, he wrapped his arm around my waist and dragged me close, claiming me as if I were a prize. His lips collided with mine, giving me the most passionate kiss, I've ever felt. It took my breath away, and I was sure if he wasn't holding me, I would have fallen. When we broke, he pushed my hair behind my ear and stared into my eyes.

"Never again. Never again will I lose you; do you understand?"

I gulped the dry air and nodded.

He smiled once more and kissed me again. "Good, let's go."

I grinned and we walked hand and hand back to my rental.

The car ride was silent until, Peter cleared his throat and said, "I'm sorry about my parents. They're so damn backwards on their views. Please know that I'm nothing like them. I love you."

"Thank you, Peter, and don't worry, I know you are nothing like that. The way you defended me, shows me that you are a different person than you were ten years ago." I replied, watching him drive.

Just by looking at his posture, I could tell that he was equally upset like me. They weren't even being rude to him, but it looked like he took equal share of the abuse. Watching the man, he'd become telling his parents off showed me that he'd changed. Becca was right all along, he was longer a boy, but a man.

"Peter?"

"Yeah?"

"What you said back there. About loving me and being in love with me regardless of my skin color. Is all of it true? It wasn't some sort of show or..."

"Mariah. I've been in love with you since that bus ride back from Forrest Lee High. Do you remember? That afternoon, we just cuddled in the seat together, listening to 50 Cent. That was the happiest I've been in a while. Right there, I knew that there's no other woman so for me."

"You were only eighteen. You had your whole life. In front of you."

"When you know, you know, Mariah. I want you. I've always wanted you."

Hearing his words and seeing his actions sparked a fire in my chest. I wanted him. The feelings were still there. The physical attraction was still there. Every inch of me wanted to touch him, to feel him, to kiss him. Without thinking, I said, "Pull over into Regency Park."

"Mariah, it's after sundown. It's closed."

"I know, but I'm about five seconds away from ripping your fucking clothes off."

Peter smiled and rose an eyebrow. He must have felt the heat that was radiating between us because he pulled into the parking lot of the park like lightning and was all over me. Our lips pressed together, and our clothes were shed instantly. He ripped away my sweater and I popped open his shirt. Feeling his hands rub my breasts through my bra made my entire body tremble. I could feel the tension build between us. I wanted him. He wanted me.

Without our lips breaking, I hiked up my skirt up and removed my panties. Peter leaned back his chair giving me extra room to hop over and unbuckled his pants. Within seconds I was sitting on his hard cock, riding him like a horse. The penetration felt amazing as I moaned from the sensual feeling. Wrapping my arms around his neck, I slowly ground myself on his crotch. His hands cupped my bare ass, and I felt his fingers grip my skin tightly. Our breathing quickened, and our eyes caught each other's as we found ourselves in locked in a heated passion. He groaned as I shifted my body on top of his and our lips reacquainted with each other, kissing as if it was our last time. Our slow dance was loving in nature. We didn't fuck like a horny hookup, but instead we made love like two long lost lovers.

Feeling his cock made my thighs quake and my back wet with sweat. I had never felt something like this before. I've had sex before, but nothing like this. Nothing could beat this. The feeling was erotic, sexy, and steamy. We both knew that we could be caught at any moment, but ten years of pent-up sexual tension was being released in the car and we had no plans on stopping it.

I could feel my pussy tighten my breathing increased until my muscles gave away and I came loudly. Peter experienced his orgasm next, releasing his seed inside me. Ordinary, I would have scolded a person doing this, but with Peter it felt right. If I were to be pregnant, I would want a baby with him. Hell, I wouldn't love to spend the rest of my life with him.

As we both got dressed, we both giggled and smiled at our rushed first time together. Peter grinned, "I can't believe that happened."

"Neither can I. Oh, my god, if Becca could see me now."

"Yeah, I'm sure that would make in hell of a story," Peter laughed.

"God, I miss her." I looked out the window, feeling guilty that I missed out on a different life.

"Hey," Peter grabbed my hand and kissed it. "I miss her too, but she did the greatest thing a best friend could ever do. She got us back together."

"Yeah, she did."

"I love you Mariah. I'm so happy that you're in my life."

"I love you too, Peter." We both stared into each other's eyes until I gave him a big smile. "Now are we going keep talking about how much we love each other or are we going to continue to have sex? I seem to recall that I have a hotel room that we could share. I'm up for round two if you are."

"Always."

Epilogue

Becca played with the scrambled eggs Peter gave her as she sat in the highchair. She looked so cute with her curly hazel hair in pigtails. I smiled at my husband cooking bacon wearing a kiss the chef apron. After kissing, Becca on the cheek I sat down at the table with a bright smile on my face.

"Good morning, babe."

"Morning, Mariah. Papers on the table if you want to read it. Coffee?"

"Yes, please." I said opening the newspaper to the business section.

Peter placed a cup of coffee on the table and smiled at my husband of two years. "Thanks, babe."

"Anytime. Bacon will be ready in a couple of minutes."

I nodded and resumed reading. As I read, I heard Becca make a noise and I placed my paper down to see that she was blowing raspberries. I laughed and joined in pushing my tongue through my lips and copied her. She laughed and made the sound louder. I smiled at our daughter as she was full of amazement from the noise that we were creating. Locked in our own world, Peter's phone went off.

"Mom? Is everything already?"

My heart fell. Since our dinner two years ago, Peter rarely ever spoke to his parents. They were unhappy about our marriage and even unhappier about our unexpected pregnancy occurring nine months after we got together. I didn't take a genius to know Becca was conceived the night we had sex in the car. Miracles happen everyday and she was our miracle.

Watching Peter talk to his parents made me nervous as he usually ended his conversations with them in a screaming match, but this time his call was different. When he hung up the phone, he had a large smile on his face.

"They want to visit with us and meet Becca."

"Are you serious?"

"Yeah. Believe it or not, my mom says that her and dad are sorry for the way that they've acted the last two years. They want to come and bury the hatchet."

I was nervous on agreeing to allow the McRoys to visit but in my heart, I knew it was best for Becca to meet her grandparents, so I agreed they could stay the weekend.

Two weeks later, watching their car pull my driveway the old feeling returned. Watching them walk out the car and hug their son, I felt my heartbeat faster than it ever had before. I watched Becca playing with a doll and seeing her gave me strength. It reminded me that all of this time, Peter stayed true to his word that night he told his parents off. He loved me with all of his heart, not once did he turn his back on me. That thought alone made me smile. I knew that what ever stood in our way we will be strong. The three of us could do anything.

The door opened and the minute his parents saw me, they scooped me up and gave me a giant hug. It caught me off guard as I was embraced by his parents. It was the exact opposite from the reaction I got before.

"Mariah! We're so sorry for the way we acted. These past years we've learned that our actions were wrong. We want to be in your lives. We want to be in our granddaughter's life. Could you find it in your heart to forgive us?"

I bit my lip and nodded. "Family is family. No matter their skin color or their past transgressions. I would love to have you both in our lives."

My in-laws smiled, clapped for joy, and hugged me once more. "Could we possibly see our granddaughter?" They asked.

"Of course. You're family now." We smiled at each other and I lead them towards Becca knowing that this was a start of a brand new wonderful life.

Secret Admirer

I hated Valentine's Day. Every year was the same. I got to see happy couples kiss, hug, and all of that other bullshit. I was tired of it all. Where was my romantic partner? Where was that guy who was going to sweep me off my feet?

Don't get me wrong, I've had my share of boys. That's right, I'm calling them *boys*, because using the word men would be too gracious of a complement. All of the boys I've dated always wanted one thing, and let's be honest that part is fun, but can't there be a man out there who wants that but always wants long walks on the beach or surprise gifts?

I guess I just wanted more. I blame the romance book industry. They fill our heads up with these perfect men, and in reality, there's no such thing.

To make my lonely Valentine's Day even worse, I have to work this Monday.

Ugh.

Pressing the button to the elevator, the machine dinged, and the doors parted. Walking in, I pressed the twenty third floor and waited for the doors to close.

As they closed, I heard someone yell, "hold the door!"

I quickly stuck my hand out and the doors parted just in time. Seconds later, my coworker, Brian McAdams stepped in.

"Thanks for getting the door, Lisa."

"You're welcome." I grinned.

He returned the smile and pressed the button for level twenty-four. We both stood in silence as the elevator shot up the high rise. Looking at Brian, he looked like typical white boy. Greased back brown hair, blue button-down long sleeves shirt and tan khakis. He was cute, but personally I could never see myself with a man like him.

For one, he's white and from my understanding white guys only liked white, Asian or Latina women. Black women are rarely included in their typical pursuit and judging by the good looks of Brian I was surely in last place in the pecking order.

I didn't know much about him other than he worked in IT. He was my personal superhero because the system at our company sucked, and it always crashed when I was using it. I'm sure he grew tired of always having to come to my cubicle to bail me out. Other than those brief moments of talking about my distaste of technology did we really talk.

"Did you have a good weekend?" He asked.

"I did. Watched Netflix. Caught up on some college basketball what about you?"

"I had a good weekend as well. I watched that UNC and Duke game. Whoa, was that a crazy game."

"Wasn't it! Two overtimes. I was glued to my seat the entire time."

"So was I. My dad went to UNC, so we're happy that the Tar Heels won."

"Oh boo!"

"What?"

"I went to Duke. Now that you told me that, I'm really don't like you now."

Brian laughed. "Hey, now."

"What else did you get into, beside cheering for the wrong team?"

"Well, my dad and me went fishing."

"Ahh, that's sweet. Did you catch a lot of fish?"

He laughed. "No, not really. We tossed most of it back. Honestly going fishing is just an excuse to go drink beer."

I laughed. "You know what, I would like that."

"You should check out Riverside Park. Lots of good fishing holes."

"Really? I would have to make a note of it."

The doors dinged and parted. "Well, that's my floor." I grinned.

"Have a good day. Oh, and happy Valentine's Day."

"Yeah, Happy Valentine's Day to you too." I waved goodbye and then walked on my floor.

I worked in the finance department of the company so most of the desks on this floor were cubicles. As I walked through the rows of gray walls, I made it to my desk and was surprised to see a large bouquet of red roses. I gasped looking at the beautiful flowers.

"Wow, oh my..." I stuttered.

At first, I thought the flowers were for someone else as I search around my office. There was no way that a guy would send me these. There had to be a mix up. I saw my coworker, Keshia, and pulled her aside.

"Hey, did someone put these on my desk by mistake?"

Keshia shook her head. "No, you missed the delivery guy. We had to sign for you on that. Let me just say that every woman here is giving you daggers right now. Whichever man you have, you better hold on to him tight. Because there's a lot of women here looking."

I stared at my coworker speechless and after she left, I quickly sat down at my desk and read the card attached to the bouquet.

Roses are red. Violets are blue. I wrote this special card for you.

You may not know who I am, but I know who you are.

You are special to me, and I plan on proving myself to you.

Will you take these roses, as a token of my love?

Love,

Your Secret Admirer

My heart leaped reading those words. I quickly read the message again and again. I couldn't believe it was real. Did someone have a crush on me? I wondered whom it could be as I scanned all the guys on my floor.

Could it be Ty? I wondered, watching him laugh with my boss. Ty was a good-looking black man, however, he was a well known womanizer in the office as he's slept with several of the women in the office. I thought about asking him if he sent me the flowers, but I remembered the note said that my admirer would reach out to me by the end of the day. So, I sighed and told myself to let the surprise come to me.

Turns out that was a bad idea as most of my morning was filled with me thinking who my mystery man could be. I was in a haze. It was a warm bubbly feeling. I'd never felt this way before on Valentine's Day. Around eleven am, the mail cart came through our floor. I rarely ever got anything, so I was surprised when the mail carrier tapped my shoulder.

"Lisa Johnson?"

"That's me." I replied, turning my chair around from my computer. My eyes open wide at the package in his hands. It was a large box of snickers, my favorite candy. Attached to the box was another note signed by my secret admirer.

Once the mail carrier left, my coworker, Keshia, popped her head out of her cubicle.

"What did you get?"

"A box of chocolates."

"What! From whom?" She exclaimed.

"My secret admirer. There's a note attached to the box too."

"Well, what are you waiting for. Read it!"

"Okay," I grinned. My fingers were full of electricity as I ripped open the envelope. I opened the card and a gift card to Chipotle fell out. I looked at the gift card and wondered what good deed I did to get blessed with these gifts. I cleared my throat and read the note.

"Dear Lisa. You're halfway through the day! Here is something sweet for the sweetest person on earth. I know how much you love chocolate. We've talked about it all the time. Enjoy lunch on me today. The gift card is to your favorite place, Chipotle. There's thirty dollars on there so feel free to invite a friend to lunch. I can't wait to express my love to you later today. Love, your secret admirer." I read.

"Oh, my god! That's so romantic!" Keshia squealed.

"You think so?" I asked.

"No, trust me. Men don't do this. I'll be lucky if my boyfriend gets flowers for me. For most couples, Valentine's Day is a mundane day, but this guy gets it. He gets the romance; he gets the magic of the day. It's amazing. Who do you think it is? He wrote that you chatted at the vending machine."

"Considering that I go to the vending machine daily and see almost everyone there, it doesn't really narrow down the list."

"Oh, damn. Hmm, I wonder who it could be?" Keshia wondered out loud as she looked around the office.

I smiled, but didn't pay any attention to her, as I looked down at the gifts that I'd received from him. Keshia was right. This guy was special. Just thinking about who it could be made my heart flutter.

"You're right. I should be happy about this."

Keshia turned her head back to me and her eyes widened in excitement. "Right? Now who are you going to Chipotle with? I'm starving right now."

I rolled my eyes. "Girl, come on."

She squealed and followed me out of the office to get lunch. During lunch all we talked about was who my mystery man could be. We managed to get a list of eligible bachelors at our company down. The list hovered around twenty names, but personally I really didn't want to date some of them. Don't get me wrong, I'm not shallow, but some men just aren't right for me.

After lunch, we started working again, well, I attempted to. As before my mind was thinking about my man of mystery. At three in the afternoon, a food delivery person walked on our floor.

"I got a hot white chocolate mocha for Lisa!"

"That's me!" I shouted. "But there must be some mistake. I didn't order anything."

The guy shrugged. "Someone paid for it. It's yours."

"Thanks," I replied taking it. I wondered who could've known that a white chocolate mocha was my favorite drink until I saw what was written on the cup. I smirked reading the message.

To Lisa

Roses are red. Violets are blue. Here's a coffee for you.
I can't wait to see you tonight.
Here's your favorite perk to keep you up tonight.

Love,

Your Secret Admirer

I giggled and took a sipped off the sweet beverage. I couldn't explain why, but this coffee tasted better than usual.

"Who's the coffee from?" Keshia asked.

"I'll give you one guess."

"No way! Damn girl, you're making me think about leaving my man for him. If you don't date him, I will!" She remarked.

I laughed and looked down at the cup. Keshia was right. Whoever this mystery man was he was hitting all the right notes.

The rest of my day, my mind was filled with thoughts of who my secret admirer could be. I barely could focus on my work as every second my mind kept drifting to who would surprise me at the end of the day.

At my job, I was usually the last one to leave for the day. As my day ended, I stretched in my cubicle and began packing up my laptop to head home, as I did, I heard a noise and I jumped. I wasn't expecting anyone on this floor, as I was the only one in the finance department still working after nine at night.

"Hello?" I asked.

"It's me," Brian's voice called out.

"Oh, hey Brian. What are you doing on this floor?"

"I came downstairs to give your gift."

"My gift?"

"Yeah, as your secret admirer, I just want to present myself to you as your final gift."

My eyes opened wide staring at him.

"It was you!"

He smiled and nodded. "Guilty. I really like you, and I would love to go on a date with you."

"Brian..." I stuttered. "How come you ever told me?"

He shrugged. "I guess I was shy. I made a promise to myself to take chances this year. One of them was to ask you out."

"Ahh, Brian, that's so sweet."

He smiled and combed his fingers through his brown hair. I could see his cheeks turn red as he blushed.

"So..." he began to say. "About dating you...did you perhaps want to go to the movies this Friday?"

"I would love to."

He smiled. "Cool, I'll see you soon." He turned and began walking away, as I watched him, I realized that I wanted this man now. I didn't want to wait. I was tired of waiting. This man swept me off my feet and all I wanted was him.

"Brian, wait!"

He turned and I rushed into his arms. I can't explain why, but I kissed him. He leaned back from my passionate embrace, but he didn't push me away. He cradled me in his arms as he accepted my gift. We both moaned and our hands explored each other both discovering the new love we shared.

It was erotic. It was sexy. It was hot. It was everything you wanted it to be in a first kiss. His breath tasted like mint as my tongue entered his mouth. I slid my tongue over his and I could hear him groan. He clutched me tightly as if he'd let go, he'd never get to hold me again.

As I pressed up against him, I felt his stiffness rub on my hip. My eyes opened wide as I pulled away from his mouth to stare at him.

Embarrassment flooded his face as he looked back at me. "Sorry, about that."

"Don't be. It's fine," I grinned. I grabbed his collar and dragged him closer to me. I pressed my lips on to his and my hand lowered to this harden cock. I rubbed the outline of it, and he groaned.

"Lisa, wait, are you sure?"

"I am. I like you too, Brian. Really, I do. Those times in the elevator are always special to me. It's Valentine's Day and I need to give you a present."

"Okay." He grinned. This thumb rubbed my cheek and my body shuddered. He leaned close to me and kissed me once more. This kiss was different than the ones before it. It was filled with hope and love. It made my heart flutter and made me moan.

My fingers felt like they were full electricity. Desire burned in my chest as I hastily unbuttoned his shit. His fingers were on my blouse as he removed my shirt was well.

I felt his fingers unclasp my bra, revealing my breasts to him.

His eyes widened at my naked state, and he leaned forward, sucking my nipple. Feeling his warm tongue brush across my teat, my body convulsed. I couldn't control the natural urges that my body went through. I leaned my head back, holding the back of Brian's head as he sucked my boob.

"Oh, Brian," I moaned.

I felt his hands reach down to my skirt. He grabbed my dress and hiked it up. He yanked away my panties and I felt the cool air dance across my skin. His fingers seemed to have a mind of their own as they drifted to my wet core. As soon as I felt them enter, I was putty in his hands.

I didn't know what was happening. One moment, Brian was revealing his love for me, the next I was sitting on the desk, with Brian's head in between my legs.

I've gotten oral before, but this was different. This was aggressive, yet passionate. It was almost primal as he took me. Lick after lick, he slurped up my juices like it was nutrients. As his tongue explored my folds, all I could do was moan. I rubbed my neck as wave after wave of pleasure crashed into me.

I never felt this way with man before, but I was loving every second of it. Brian's tongue circled around my clit, and that's when I lost all motor function. I was in full auto, as my body climaxed. I couldn't calm down as my body shook involuntarily.

Fuck.

As I came down from my ultimate high, Brian stood back up, he rubbed my cheek as he stared into my eyes.

"I want you." I begged; my voice heavy with need.

"I don't have a condom."

"It's fine. I'm on birth control. I want to do this here. Do you?"

"More than ever." He leaned forward and kissed me once more as we kissed, he positioned himself in between my legs. I heard his belt unbuckle and his pants hit the floor. Soon I felt his dick inside me, and I moaned. I clutched him close as he thrusted in an out of me. My legs crossed around his back as he fucked me.

Both of us were full of grunts and moans. Having him take me in the office was so unprofessional but it was the hottest thing I ever did.

"How does that feel?" He groaned.

"It feels good. Just like that. Just like that." I repeated holding on to his bare ass. That damn thing was all muscle and it felt like I was holding on to a bucking bronco.

Goddamn, his did his dick feel good. For a white guy, I didn't expect much, but I was wrong. He was long and thick and knew exactly how to use it. He was hitting places that I didn't even know were there.

"Oh, Lisa," he moaned. He looked me in the eyes before his lips crashed into mine again. I love kissing him. There's something about how soft his lips felt. I can't explain it. It's hard to put it to words.

My hands shifted to his neck and his hands lowered from my thighs to my ass. He picked me up and carried me to a nearby chair. He sat down, allowing me to ride him.

We were in sync. He didn't even have to tell me what he wanted. I knew he wanted me to ride him and that's what I did. I bounced on his cock, moaning as I hit my climax yet again.

Sweat poured from my forehead as our strenuous session continued. He held my ass as I rode him to completion. His mouth opened wide as he groaned, and I soon felt him cum inside me. That feeling of him finishing set me off once more as I sung my praises.

When we were done, we sat quietly looking into each other's eyes. He cupped my cheek and smiled.

"Happy Valentine's Day," he whispered.

"Happy Valentine's Day," I grinned. "I really enjoyed my gifts."

"I did too."

I laughed. "Yeah, I felt it."

He joined in on my laughed and leaned forward to kissed me once more. As we kissed, I knew that this was the start of something new, and I was right it was the start of something. After several months of dating, Brian popped the question to me and we got married, years later we had kids. Through it all, I still remember how he became my secret admirer giving me the most special Valentine's Day present I've ever received.

The Football Player
Chapter 1

I never thought I'd fall for a white guy. Let's be honest, growing up around black men, I'd just assumed that I'd only date black men. The neighborhood I lived in was all black. The school I went to was all black. Even my church was all black. I was only used to one race.

It wasn't until I enrolled into Tech that my point of view changed. It was my freshman year. My best friend and roommate, Gina had dragged me out of the room to go to the club. Personally, I would have stayed in and studied on a Thursday night, Gina had other plans.

"Girl, I'm so excited that you decided to come out."

"We're only going to stay for two hours. I have a quiz tomorrow and..."

"Shit, you and I both know that you are going to Ace that quiz. I've never seen someone as smart as you are. You are in college! Live it up, girl! You are supposed to be cutting class and going out for thirsty Thursdays. You only get to go here once."

"Apparently you plan on going here forever with your grades. How is your English 101 class going again?"

"Girl!" My friend smacked her lips and rolled her eyes. "That's nuff talk about school!"

"And the point goes to Katrina." I remarked.

Gina laughed and slapped my shoulder. "You're lucky I like your ass."

I chuckled as we walked up to the club. If you would have driven by this place at night you would have assumed, it was a dump. Based on its outer windowless appearance it looked like a place crackheads would sleep in, however, at night, it was the hottest club in the city. The line was wrapped around the building as we waited to get in.

As usual, Gina and I were dressed to kill. We were both wearing mini dresses, that showed enough skin to make our pastor fall to his knees and bless us for our sins.

I'm not going to lie, I liked wearing dresses like these. I seemed to catch every single guy's eye as they walked past us to get in line. We had no problem getting into the club even though we were underage. I'm pretty sure my fake ID wasn't the best, but my other assets seemed to help the bouncer make his decision.

Inside, the music was blaring. It was loud enough to make your eardrums shake. The dance floor was crowded as girls and guys dirty danced like there was no tomorrow.

Gina nudged me and pointed to the bar. "You want a shot?"

"Yeah, let's go."

We walked up to the bar and ordered two fireball whiskey shots. The bartender poured us two drinks and Gina yelled at the woman, "Can we start a tab?"

The lady nodded and took the card from us but before she left the largest black guy I have ever seen approached us. He had a backwards grey Tech flat brim hat on along with a blue button-down shirt, jeans and boots.

"Actually, put it on my tab." The deep voiced man said.

Gina and I looked at each other and smiled back to our savior.

"Thank you!" We both chorused.

He nodded and took a sip of his mixed drink in his hand.

"I'm Lamar, that's my boy, Mike," he pointed towards an equally larger white guy. Mike was blonde with short hair. I'm not going to lie based on looks alone he looked like a beefy version of Eminem. The jeans, white thermal, and Timbs told me that he had a little hood in him.

"I'm Gina and that's Katrina."

"Hey," I waved.

Lamar gave us a head nod, but his vision seemed to hover around Gina making me her shadow. That was something Mike and I shared in common as we both awkwardly looked at each other.

Gina and Lamar seemed to be hitting it off well as they both flirted with one another. Through their comments, I learned that Mike and Lamar were both on the football team. However, it didn't take a Phd to figure out they played sports. Both were stacked like mountains.

"Are you having a good time?" I asked Mike.

He nodded.

I grinned, "you're not a very talkative person, are you?"

He shook his head. "I get nervous around beautiful woman."

I looked down as my ears became warm. I knew that line shouldn't have worked on me, but I'm not going to lie, it felt good to hear it. They way he looked at me gave me shivers. I'm not talking about a gawking stare where he's undressing you with his eyes. No, this was something larger than that. The way he looked at me made me feel like I was the only woman in the world. I was his queen and he lived to serve me. I didn't see I coming, but it certainly took the air out of my lungs.

I nodded towards the dance floor, "did you want to dance?"

A large smile spread on his face as he nodded and grabbed my hand leading me. As we walked away, I shouted, "Gina! I'm dancing with Mike!"

My friend didn't seem to care was she waved me off.

I was surprised at how good Mike danced. He knew most of the moves and we were both looking like two backup dancers as we broke it down. I'm not sure how long we spent dancing. All I knew was I was hot and sweaty, and I needed a break. I tapped his shoulder and he stopped dancing.

"Hey, did you want to get some air? It's hotter than hell in here."

"Yeah, I would like that."

We both walked outside and there was a bar out there, along with several chairs for us to sit. The cool fall air felt great on my warm skin as I inhaled the fresh air.

"Did you want something to drink?" He asked.

"Yeah, I'll take Sex on the Beach."

"What?" His eyes went wide.

I laughed. "You never heard of that drink?"

"That's a drink?"

I laughed even harder that time. "Yeah, it is. Just trust me. Go to the bar and order one."

He nodded and walked back to the bar. He came back with two crimson cups filled with the orange juice tequila cocktail.

"Do you get one too?" I asked.

"I wanted some sex on the beach," he mocked.

"Oh my…" I snorted laughing again. "Just the way you said that makes me feel dirty."

"Yeah, it's a fun name for a drink. Is it good?" He asked, raising the glass.

"Yeah, it's good. Trust me." He handed me the drink and rose the glass.

"Cheers."

"Cheers." He replied, clashing my drink with his.

I took one sip of the drink and moaned as my taste buds reacted to the fresh orange juice. "Mmm, do you like it?"

"Yeah, it's not too bad."

"Right?" I took another sip. "So, tell me about yourself, Mike."

"I'm a freshman, I start on the team as the quarterback."

"Oh, you must be really good to start on the team as a freshman."

"Thanks, I was a five-star recruit coming out of high school."

"What is that supposed to mean?"

"Oh, it means that I was one of the best athletes in the nation."

"That's cool. How are you playing so far?"

"Good, I'm like a phenomenon right now. Everyone is already talking about me making it to the pros."

"Really?"

"Yeah, I'm surprised you didn't notice me. Usually everyone sees me out in the crowd."

"Yeah, I don't watch a lot of football."

"What! You have to come to my game."

"Ugh...I would rather be studying."

"Oh, come on. You should come. I can get you good seats. Please come to my game."

"Alright, I'll come." I grinned.

"Cool," he smiled. "So, what are you studying?"

"Oh, I want to be a doctor. So, I'm a pre-Med."

"Oh, that's dope. So, you're super smart?"

I shrugged. "I wouldn't say super smart. I just know my stuff. What are you studying?"

"I'm studying communications."

"Communications? Isn't that like a broad major? What did you want to do with that, I mean how are you going to use that degree if football doesn't work out?"

"Huh, I never really thought of that. I mean I take it because they tell me it's an easy course to get an A."

"Oh, sorry, I didn't mean to barge like that. Damn I sound like my parents."

"You're parents strict?"

"The strictest. They are both doctors and want me to become one too. I'm pretty sure if I fail, they will disown me."

Mike laughed. "Yeah, I know the feeling."

"Really?" I rose my eyebrows.

"Yeah, well not in school but in football. My dad played in the NFL and he has the same career goals for me as well. He pushes me to be good at this sport. I feel like if I don't win the national championship this year, he may disown me too."

I laughed and his eyes widened at my random outburst.

"I'm sorry, I know we are supposed to be having this heart to heart right now, but I just realized that by disappointing our parents we would both be homeless."

"Huh, yeah, that is sort of funny if you look at it like that. Well, if you get kicked out, you can always crash at my place." He admitted.

"Aw, that's sweet, well if you get kicked out, you can sleep on the floor in my dorm room. However, I'm not sure if they let guys sleep there."

"Nah, we'll make it work." He joked with a large grin. Damn, I loved that man's smile.

I laughed again. I couldn't explain why but I couldn't stop smiling at Mike. It could have been the drinks or the company, but he was so down to earth that I didn't even realize that we talked for an hour. We gelled so easy and had a lot in common, in regard to movies, music, and personalities.

Throughout the night we sat closer and closer together to the point that I didn't even realize that I was cuddling underneath his arm when Gina came stomping back.

"Huh! There you are!" She snapped.

Mike and I shared a look.

"Are you okay?" I asked. I could tell she was upset about something. The fact that Lamar wasn't nearby wasn't a good sign.

She crossed her arms, smacked her lips and glared at Mike as if he was the cause of her terrible night. "Lamar was an asshole by the way. The moment I turned my back, he was all over another woman." Mike opened his mouth in protest, but Gina ignored him and turned her glare towards me. "I'll watch out for him." She hissed pointing at Mike.

Mike's jaw dropped as he was accused of doing something he didn't do. I was a bit surprised too, as my conversation with Mike was good. Not once did his eyes stray or did he want to talk to someone else.

"Gina, Mike's been chill actually."

My friend rolled her eyes. "I'm leaving the club. This place is dead anyways. Are you coming with me or not?"

I looked back at Mike. I didn't want the night to end there. Call me crazy, but I actually felt something with him. There was a connection with him that I wanted to explore. Perhaps it was selfish of me, but I really wanted to explore that connection with him. However, in the end, Gina was my girl, and I had to make sure she got home safe.

I sighed and looked back at Mike. "I'm sorry, but I have to go."

"It's a'ight. I had a good time with you. Hey, can I get your number? I would love to talk to you more."

"Yeah, I would like that. Where's your phone?" I asked.

He handed me his smartphone and I sent myself a text message.

"I just texted myself. That's my number."

"Oh, cool. Text me when you get home safe, okay?"

"Yeah, I will."

I stood up and walked away with Gina. As I walked away with her, I looked back and stared at Mike. He looked like a kicked puppy with his bright blue eyes. Damn I wanted to give him a hug. I couldn't explain it, but that feeling that I felt with him was like no other. It was a burning desire to be close to him and I promised myself to see it out.

Mike and I texted all the time. It could be any time of the day or night and my phone would randomly buzz, and every time it did a smile would appear on my face. He loved sending me funny gifs that made me laugh throughout the day. Honestly any text from him was the highlight of my day. On Friday night, I got a ping from him, and I couldn't help but to grin from ear to ear when I read it.

Mike: Hi beautiful

Damn, whenever he posts messages like that my heart melts.

Me: Hey. How was practice?
Mike: It was good. We are going to go through one more meeting before we call it a night. I just wanted to text you real quick. Did you get the tickets for the game I sent you?
Me: I did. You gave me too many though.
Mike: Those are for anyone you want to bring. Parents, friends, ex boyfriends to show how cool I am.

I laughed loudly and Gina gave me a death glare from her laptop. She wasn't fond of my new relationship with Mike. In a way, I think she was jealous as her and Lamar didn't work out. However, I didn't care, what Mike and I shared was special.

I never felt this way about a man before. In high school, relationships were more of a status symbol. A girl goes out with a guy because he's popular or vice versa, but what Mike and I were building was something different. It was something you'd only see in romance movies or read about in romance books.

It's hard to describe. I don't want to call it an addiction because that's usually has the stigma of something bad, and what Mike and I had wasn't bad. Call it young love for falling head over heels. I'm not sure, but what I was sure about was that he had trapped me in his love web, and I didn't want to get out.

Me: You're the only one I care to see.
Mike: Same here. Hey question for you, after my game, did you want to go to the club again? I would love to go dancing with you.
Me: Yeah, I would like that.
Mike: See you soon. I got to get ready to the game. I can't wait to see you again.
Me: Me either. See you soon.

After texting him, I sighed, and a large smile grew on my face. I couldn't stop thinking of Mike.

Gina noticed my gleeful expression and placed her hand on her hip.

"You talking to Mike again?"

"How do you know?"

"You get this dizzy look in your eyes."

"Oh," I laughed and shrugged. "Yeah. I was."

"You really like him, huh?" She asked.

"I do. He's a really great guy. I can't believe I'm falling for a white guy, but we have so much in common it's crazy."

"I'm happy for you. I truly am, but just watch out for him. He's a football player. These guys want only one thing."

"Mike's not like that."

"You sure about that?" Gina asked. "As soon as some other girl flaunts her shit in front of your new man, how is he going to act?"

"Mike has had plenty of chances to bounce. He's stuck with me."

"Sure. You'll see. Just when you get your heart broken, don't come crying to me." Gina shook her head and walked out of our dorm room.

I shouldn't have taken her words so heavily, but I did. Like a cloud her words hung over me. All throughout the weekend our conversation replayed in my mind. What if Mike wasn't the guy he said he was?

Part of me didn't want to believe it. He was a really sweet down to earth guy. If you would have spoken to him, you would have never guessed he was some amazing freshman phenomenon quarterback. While the other part of me, knew what Gina said held truth. He was a guy and let's face it, that thing in between their legs has a mind of its own.

That Saturday, Mike got my friends and I great seats on the fifty-yard line. I was amazed watching Mike play in in pads. I didn't think I could be so attracted to the man before. His muscles...Damn. That's all I have to say.

They won the game easily. Mike couldn't be stopped as he threw multiple touchdowns. It was great high-fiving people and telling them that I know him. I felt like a small celebrity myself.

Later that night, I got dressed go met him at the club. I opted for a mini black dress, with heels and hoop earrings. As I prepared myself to go out, my roommate Gina stared at me.

"Are you sure you want to do this?" She asked.

I nodded. "He's a good guy, Gina."

"I just don't want you getting hurt."

"I won't. I promise." I smiled at her and gave her a big hug.

I took a taxi downtown and found Mike waiting outside the club. The moment he saw me his eyes went bigger than saucers.

"Katrina..." he breathed as his eyes went from north to south. It felt like I was watching the man's soul leave his body as he ogled me.

He didn't look to bad himself. He was wearing a blue collared shirt with a pair of jeans and boots. The way he rolled his sleeves to display his forearm muscles created a fire in my belly. Like him, I was in awe.

"Katrina! You're here." He grinned. He opened his arms wide and gave me a hug. It felt great to feel his warm embrace. Call me crazy, but I wanted more. For those few seconds wrapped up in his arms I felt this magical romantic tingle spread throughout my body. When we broke apart, we both stared into each other eyes, waiting for one of us to talk.

"I really enjoyed your game. You played well." I grinned.

"Thanks. I can't explain it, but having you there just made me want to play better. Are you ready to go in?"

"Yeah, let's go."

I followed him into the club, and we had no trouble getting in. Once again, I felt like a VIP with Mike as everyone knew him. Everyone gave him a high five and dabbed him up.

"Did you want to go dance or get a drink first?" He asked.

"Dance," I grinned.

He smiled and grabbed my hand as we walked to the center. Unlike last time, we didn't dance separately. We were all over each other grinding our bodies together to the beat. It felt good to have him close to me. I loved the way his cologne smelled. The way he touched my hips as we swung back and forth felt amazing. I could feel his excitement on my ass, only making me want him more. We danced for about an hour and sweat poured down our foreheads as we separated both taking long breaths.

"That was fun. I'm so hot though." I replied.

He nodded. "Me too, did you want something to drink?"

"Another sex on the beach." I told him.

He winked at me. "Of course." He swam through the crowd and talked to the bartender.

Standing there I waited for him to return. As I watched him, I saw how several girls went up to him and talked to him. I could tell they were flirting. The way they turned their heads and laughed at everything he said. I'm not sure why I was tripping. I knew Mike came with me to the club, but the words of Gina rung in my head. I was concerned that her words held truth. What if he truly was just out to sleep with me?

I doubt creeped into my mind until, I felt a finger tap me on the shoulder.

"Katrina, I got your drink…" he paused and studied my facial expressions. "Are you okay?" He asked.

I shook my head and walked away.

"Katrina wait!" He called out following me.

I sat outside. I'm not sure why I was getting so emotional. Was I stupid for believing this was something more, I asked myself.

"Katrina? What's wrong?" He asked.

I shook my head. "Gina was right about you."

"Right about what?"

"I saw you talking to those girls. They were all over you."

Mike sighed and nodded. "Yeah, they were. I'm not going to lie, being in the position that I am in on the football team makes me a popular person on campus. Girls are going to come up to me and hit on me. There's nothing that I can do to stop them, but I did tell them I was with you. You have to believe me when I say, if I'm with you. I'm with you. No woman would ever come between what we have."

"How do I know you're telling the truth? How do I know that this isn't some game you're playing on me like Lamar did to Gina?"

"Lamar is a *fool*, and fools push away things that are good for him. You are good for me Katrina, and I don't plan on pushing you away." He walked closer to me and held my hands.

"This past week, has been one of my best weeks of my life. I can't explain it, but talking to you has been the brightest part of my day. If I lose you..." he shook his head and looked away. "I don't know. It pains me to even think of it. We can take it slow, we can go fast. I don't *fucking* care. I just want you. I don't care how long it takes for me to prove to you have much I care about you. There aren't enough words for me to explain how much I like you. I want you. Only you."

"Mike..." I began to say.

He cupped my face with his hands and stared into my eyes. The look he gave me was like no other. It made the hairs on my back stand.

As he leaned forward, his voice was heavy with need. "Please let me prove it to you." He begged with such emotion that it made my heart swell. I could see the passion in his eyes as he stared into mine. "Please, let me show you how much I care."

My mind was at a crossroads. I didn't know what to do. Logically, I shouldn't have trusted Mike, but my heart wanted to see. My heart wanted to see what path we would fall down if I said yes. My brain took a back seat as my heart expressed what it wanted.

"Show me then..." I whispered.

That was all the permission he needed as his lips crashed into mine. He held me tightly as we kissed. I've never been kissed like that before. There was so much emotion and power behind it, that it took my breath away. I was starstruck and gasping for air. I craved more of it as my arms wrapped around his. He held me tightly as if he knew that if he'd let me go, I'll never get a chance to hold me again. Kissing him was a moment I'd never forget and when we were done, he stared into my eyes stroking my cheek.

I didn't know his plans, but I knew that I didn't plan on letting him go tonight.

"Mike?"

"Yeah?"

"Can we go back to your place?"

"I would love to." He grinned.

We could barely make it into Mike's apartment as we stumbled in. Our mouths were glued together as we kissed. Moans and groans were both being made as we shed our clothes.

I didn't plan on sleeping with Mike, but my plans were derailed after his confession. I knew that we barely knew each other but listening to him tell me how much he cared about me opened up my heart. I wanted this man. Damn the costs. Damn the consequences. Damn everything.

Taking of his shirt, I was impressed by his defined muscles. His chest looked like it was sculpted from God himself. My fingers slid down the distinct ridges of his pecks and abs and I felt my body shudder. How was it possible for one man to look like this?

Hunger for this man clouded my mind as my mouth crash into his once more. He tasted so sweet. Like sugar, all I wanted was more. I craved it.

"Oh, Katrina," he moaned.

"Mike..." I breathed.

I felt his tongue enter my mouth as his long member massaged my own. My insides were burning with desire as I hopped into his arms and dry humped him. I could feel his stiffness in his jeans as he groaned. He grabbed my ass and carried me to the bed. He laid me down gazing at me like I was an angel.

"You are so beautiful."

"Really?" I asked.

He nodded. "I am the luckiest man on earth right now."

"Prove it." I challenged.

He rose an eyebrow and replied, "as you wish."

He removed my panties and sunk below my vision. I next felt his tongue inside my wet folds, and I was putty in his hands. Holding my hips, his tongue slithered in and out of my core. I was a mess as I moaned, and my back arched. The pleasure inside me grew and grew as I held his head below.

The man was a machine. He didn't stop. He didn't complain. It was like he was the damn terminator of eating pussy. The pleasure inside me was like no other. Wave after wave took me and just when I thought I couldn't hold on much longer, I came.

The feeling was eutrophic as very positive emotion inside me was released.

"Oh, Mike," I uttered as my high rapidly spread across my body.

He looked up and cupped my face. He stared into my eyes and smiled.

"Was it good?" He asked.

"Yeah, it was." I breathed.

He chuckled. "I want you. Are you ready for me?"

"I am."

He smiled at me and reached into his nightstand. He grabbed a condom and rolled the latex down his hard shaft. My body trembled at the idea of having him inside me. He hovered his massive member above my opening and then sunk in. As he did, my toes curled, and I moaned. I held his back tightly as he penetrated me deeply.

He stretched me out like no other man had. That feeling of him being inside was nothing that I expected. He held my head and stared into my eyes. What we were sharing wasn't just sex. Dare I say it was love.

Slowly he thrust, rocking his hips back and forth. I held his ass as my legs rose higher and higher. We were in sync as he took me in the bed. Although it was just missionary position, it was the sexiest session I ever experienced. The way he held me in his arms was like no other. The feeling of his fingers sliding across my skin felt like pure electricity.

My lungs burned and my head spun as I taken out of this world. Our speed increased and soon we weren't just going slow. It was hard and fast like two pornstars. Not only was he a romantic lover, but he was also an aggressive lover and the combination of the two was like no other.

He held my legs above my head, as he pounded my pussy. I could barely even speak, yet alone think. Watching his sexy body crash into mine was like no other.

Eventually, we shifted positions. He had me on my side, with him behind me. He held my hip as he continued to rock into me. Despite the of change position, I still felt like a goddess in his hands. The way he touched me felt like he was praising me like I was an almighty deity. I loved the way he grabbed my breasts and squeezed them in his hands. I loved he way he whispered sweet messages in my ear as he took me. He was a little aggressive too as he yanked my hair back, growling as he fucked me.

All of it built my pleasure to its peak. With one gasp, I came once more. My screams vibrated off the walls as I experienced my ultimate high. Twice in one night, I was one lucky girl.

"You, okay?" He asked.

I nodded. My brain still couldn't form words yet. I wasn't to that portion of my mental reboot. I was lucky to still be breathing as this man's cock had found a way to put me in a sexually induced coma. Don't ask me how, I'm still trying to figure that out.

"Did you want to get on top?" He asked.

Once more I nodded. I was in a haze as we shifted positions. Sex with him was better than any drug. It was top notch, cream of the crop, and dynamite. However, I didn't expect to see how large he was when he pulled out of me. The man built like a bull and had the stamina of one as well.

I sat on top of him and purred as his dick stretched me out. This new position was foreign, but it felt right. Looking up to me, he grabbed my ass, and we moved our bodies as one. He smiled at me, not pulling his eyes away.

Once more we were making love. The man's hands had a mind of their own as they touched my breasts, neck, and cheeks. Each time he touched me; he gave me goosebumps. It was passionate, it was loving, it was everything you wanted your first time to be.

His blue eyes never left mine as he looked at me. This stirred my emotions up even more. This wasn't just sex to him. This was something else. It was something that only people in twenty-year relationships experience. Dare I saw it. Was it love?

I could see him wanting to say something as he held me. It was at the tip of his tongue. Hesitation held him back as he seemed to have an internal struggle.

I didn't question it, until I heard him murmur, "Katrina?"

"Yes?" I moaned.

"This time with you. In this bed...I can't describe it. I know I have my whole life to live, but in my life on this earth so far, I've never experienced anything like this. I've never experienced you."

"Oh, Mike..." I moaned.

Leaned forward and kissed him. He grabbed the side of my cheek and pushed my hair behind my ears. His eyes not once strayed from mine. It was like I was looking into his soul.

"Katrina...I love you." He admitted.

I was in shock. I didn't know what to say. We only knew each other for a week, yet he was confessing his love for me then and there.

"Mike...I..."

"I know. It's crazy. It's been a week, right? But I can't get you out of my mind. You're like some beautiful love virus that I'm infatuated with. I want you. I want all of you. I want to have you for until my dying days. You are sexy, funny, smart. I know our relationship is new, but I don't care. I don't care what others say. I want you and only you. I want this and I'm going to fight for this. Will you have me?"

Emotions swelled with in me. I didn't expect this. I didn't expect him. What do you say to a man who bared his soul to you? I wasn't crazy. What I felt wasn't strange. He felt it too. We were both in this together. Us against the world, and that was enough for me.

I smiled at him and kissed him. I could hear him moan as our lips touched. Leaning close to his ear, I finally admitted those four words to him as well.

"I love you too."

He held my chin and looked into my eyes once more. No more words were shared after that. They didn't need to be. All was shared. All was bared. We didn't have sex after that moment. We were making love. He held me tightly as he pounded into me. I moved my body with his, stoke after stroke.

Seconds later I felt myself explode. It was like every single positive I've emotion I've ever felt popped out of me. I screamed and my body went stiff as I exhaled. This orgasm was like no other and frankly speaking it was the best I'd ever experience in my life. It was a feeling of full release. Something that can't be described in words, only felt. When I was finished, I felt reborn.

Looking down, Mike followed soon after me. He groaned and he closed his eyes. He held me tightly as he finished inside me. When he was done, we rolled to our sides, and he pulled out of me. After ripping off the condom and tossing it in the trash, he cuddled up close to me and kissed me.

"I love you, Katrina. That was magical." He breathed.

I wanted to say it back, but something held my tongue. Once more the words of my roommate repeated. Once more I heard her say that, men would say or do anything to get in your pants. Was this apart of his game? Did he lie just to get me to this point? I had to know.

I grabbed his chin and stared into his deep blue eyes.

"Mike, are you sure this is what you want? Are you sure you love me? This isn't some fling to get it in? I just don't want to be hurt."

He narrowed his eyes and held my chin like he's done countless of times.

"This isn't a game. I'm all in. I don't know what else to say to you to prove to you how I love you. But isn't that love? Love is a gamble. I'm willing to pay the full price for you. Are you? I will not stray. You are mine and mine alone. You are incredibly sexy. I love your personality. I can't see myself with anyone but you. I'm in this until the end of the line. I love you and I promise you I will never break your heart."

I smiled hearing his words. He was right, love was a gamble. He was all in and I needed to be in as well. I took a deep breath knowing that there was no turning back from my next words.

"I love you too." I replied.

He grinned and kissed me once more.

This kiss was his seal. It was his signature to a promise that he never broken. Not once since that night had I'd ever doubted him. From that sensual night our romance bloomed. We stuck together all throughout college and life. I supported his football career in the pros, and he supported me getting my doctorate's. We got a big house, raised two kids together, and lived a storybook romance together. We laughed, loved, fucked, and did everything to the fullest. In the end, our love never wavered once, even if we had our spats and disagreements. At the end of the day, I knew that he loved me, and I loved him.

Sneak Preview of Claimed by my Wolf Savior

"Help me!" I screamed. My legs kicked and flailed, attempting to push off the two frat boys pinning me down. Both of them held me against my will, pushing my shoulders into the dirt of the forest. I attempted to escape, but it was no use as the pressure they applied was too great.

"Help me!" I called out again, struggling to break free.

"Shhh," one of the frat boys grinned as he stroked my cheek. "There's no one out there that can save you. We're in the middle of the woods."

Laughing, the other frat boy agreed. "Yeah, there's no one around for miles. Why do you think we decided to have a bonfire out in the woods? You should save your breath."

"Get off me!" I screamed attempting to break free.

"Would you calm down! You wanted this!"

"No, I didn't!" I snapped back.

"Please, you were eye fucking me and my friend back at that bonfire. We are simply obliging to your actions."

"Get off!" I snapped.

"Oh, come on, Yolanda. Don't be like that. You told me yourself, you always wanted to have sex with a white guy. This is your sexual fantasy, don't fight it." The creep reached below my skirt and groped my upper leg. I cried as I felt his fingers crawl up my skin to my panties. I fought back the best I could and spat into his face. He drew his hand back and glared at me, as he wiped my spit from his face.

"You fucking black cunt!" He slapped me hard across the face and I wailed as my face stung from his impact. I could feel the blood roll down my cheek as I stared at him. Grabbing his belt, the frat boy undid his pants and growled, "Hold her down, Greg."

Greg chuckled and pulled my arms out, stretching me out for the other. "After your done, I'll get a turn right, Matt? I always wanted to fuck a black chick."

"Yeah, Yeah. After…" he grinned, rubbing his white prick.

I screamed again but was gagged by Greg cupping his hand over my mouth.

"Shh…" he whispered. "The more you fight it, the worse it's going to be. It's best to sit back and enjoy it."

Matt laughed and fell to his knees. He grabbed my skirt and hiked it above my stomach. I tried to fight him off, but it was no use. He ripped away my panties, and hovered above me, stroking his white one-eyed monster. As he leaned in closer, I closed my eyes accepting my fate, waiting for the moment that I regretted the most.

However, it never came. Instead, I heard a low-pitched growl and then a horrible scream.

Was it a wild wolf? I thought opening my eyes.

My jawed dropped as I saw a black furred animal attack Matt and Greg. It was twice the size of any wolf that I saw at the zoo and moved at unnatural speeds. His black fur was shaggy, and his eyes were dark red like the devil. Both frat boys screamed as the animal ripped them to shreds. When it was done, the two corpses of Greg and Matt were laying in front of me. Their bloody carcasses, didn't move, as their glossy eyes stayed frozen in fear. When the wolf was done, it looked towards me. It's snout, painted with the crimson blood of Matt and Greg. I backed away, knowing that I would be its next victim. I waited for the fatal strike, but it never came.

Instead, the wolf whimpered and slowly walked towards me. I'm not sure what I was thinking, but I extended my hand towards the large beast and like a trained dog, it licked my hand. I smiled at the wolf from its friendly greeting.

"Thank you." I replied.

The wolf bowed his head as if it understood me.

I narrowed my eyes, confused at the sight. "Can you understand me?"

The wolf bowed its head one more.

I shook my head. "How is it possible? Wolves don't understand people."

The animal backed away from me, and then I saw something supernatural as the beast transformed right before my eyes. I watched as his wolf features disappeared and human features emerged. My mouth dropped as a naked human stood before me. He stood at around six foot and weighted twice as much as I did. His long dark hair was wild and untamed, reaching to his shoulders. He muscled body was glistening in sweat and covered by tribal tattoos. As I gazed upon his Tarzan like statue, my eyes became fixated on his exposed thick pale cock. It hung low, and while it was flaccid, it looked large in size. I knew I shouldn't have stared, but my eyes couldn't pull away from his naked body.

He cleared his throat and I looked back into his dark mysterious eyes.

"You're a...a..."

"Werewolf." He responded.

"Impossible. Werewolves don't exist." I retorted.

"We actually do. We just don't make contact with humans much."

"Wow..." I replied. I looked back at the dead men and rubbed my shoulder. "thank you for saving me."

"You're welcome. I heard you in the distance. They didn't hurt you, did they?" He stepped closer to me and inspected the mark that Matt left. As his rough fingers graced my cheek and my legs trembled from this touch. His presence alone made my heart triple its pace.

"It looks like just a flesh wound. You should be fine with time."

"Thanks," I replied.

"Well, I must be going. If you walk a mile East," he said pointing towards the right. "There's a gas station. You should be able to dial for help there."

"Wait! Can't you take me there?"

He shook his head. "I've already done more than I should. I must be going and catch up to my pack. They are waiting for me."

He turned and began to walk away before I caught his hand. "Wait!"

"Is everything alright?" he asked.

"It's just I wanted to repay you. You saved me."

"No payment is necessary."

"At least give me your name."

He looked away and bit his lip. I could tell that he was hesitant on telling me. "It's Anton."

"Yolanda." I replied, touching my chest.

About the Author

Jada Washington is a new aspiring author that loves to write about sizzling BWWM romances. If she's not writing, she is enjoying time with her family and two Serbian huskies. Outside of writing, her hobbies include biking, swimming and traveling.

Follow me on Twitter!

@JadaWasAuthor